Big Annie

An American Tall Tale

Adapted by Sandra Robbins
Illustrated by Iku Oseki

This book has a companion Read-Along/Move-Along audio tape.
Available from See-More's Workshop, 325 West End Avenue NY, NY 10023

Big Annie was 6 feet 8 inches tall
and weighed 300 pounds. She lived in New Orleans
at the mouth of the Mississippi River.
Big Annie was a flatboat captain.
A flatboat is a barge without an engine of its own.
Annie's friend, Captain Jim, would pull her barge up
the river with his tugboat from New Orleans to Natchez.

Big Annie loved to sing while she worked.
The children who lived along the winding river's edge
would sing along too.

Every year, early in December, Big Annie waited
for a ship that sailed across the ocean. It carried Christmas
toys from Paris, France for Annie to bring to the children
in the town of Natchez.

One year the ship did not come.
For days Big Annie paced the dock.
By the day before Christmas, Annie was really worried.
"If the ship isn't here today," Big Annie said,
"the children will never get their presents
in time for Christmas Day."

Annie's friends, the birds and the fish,
were waiting too. The fish jumped high and
the birds flew overhead
looking for the white sails.
In the early morning light,
Annie sent them out to the ocean
to see if that ship
was coming in.

Big Annie sang to her friends.

"Little fish swim and tell me,
Birds fly high up in the sky.
See if the toys are coming,
If that ship is coming by.
Go as fast as you can swim,
Go as fast as you can fly,
See if that ship is anywhere about."

With tails splashing and wings flapping,
off they went.

At last they saw the ship
with its striped French flag flying.
The fish jumped in the waves
as they swam back.
The birds filled the morning air
with their calling sounds
telling Big Annie the good news.

"Annie, we see it near
We see the ship, we see the toys,
We see it clear.

Annie, it's on its way.
The ship is here, the time is now.
Oh, what a day!"

With sails billowing in the wind,
the ship pulled into shore.

"Hurry up! Unload that ship,"
Big Annie said. "The children
are a-waitin' in the town of Natchez."

The Captain quickly lowered
the gangplank onto Big Annie's barge.
Down came teddy bears and tricycles,
red wagons and bicycles,
and all kinds of wonderful toys.

Just as they finished loading her flatboat,
Big Annie heard the storm bells clanging.
Everyone stopped to listen.
A storm was brewing on the Mississippi River.
The birds and the fish
could hardly believe their ears.

They called, "Annie, you can't go.
You can't take your barge
up the river in a storm."

"I have no time to worry about that.
Here comes my friend Captain Jim."

"Captain Jim, c'mon, we're Natchez bound!
The ship's in from Paris, turn your boat around.
Children are a-waitin', it will be a great day!
Toys we'll be a-bringin', let's get on our way."

Captain Jim shrugged his shoulders and said,

"No, Big Annie, can't you hear the bells a-ringin'?
There's a storm there a-brewin'
and you cannot get through.
The winds are a-blowin'
right up the Mississippi,
No, Ma'am Annie, I'm not comin' with you!"

All the boats on the river blew their horns.

"Toot! Toot! Annie, what'cha gonna do now?
Toot! Toot! Annie, what'cha gonna do?
Toot! Toot! Annie, what'cha gonna do now?
There's a storm there a-brewin'
and you cannot get through!"

"Well, then, I'll just have to find someone else," she said.
"Here comes Captain John."
But Captain John held on tight to his paddle wheel
and said,

"No, Big Annie, there's a storm out there a-brewin',
No, Big Annie, can't you hear the whistle blow!
The winds are a-blowin' right up the Mississippi,
No, Ma'am Annie, I just won't go!"

"I guess I'll have to
find someone with a
horse and cart to pull me
up the side of the river. Here
comes Mister Jackson."

But Mister Jackson said, "Sorry,
Captain Annie. With those rains a-comin'
there's gonna be mud
from here to Natchez."

"Don't you know, Annie,
up there it's a-rainin',
Don't you know, Annie,
the roads are washed out.
The winds are a-blowin'
right up the Mississippi,
No, Ma'am Annie, can't help you out!"

Once again all the boats on the river blew their horns.

"Toot! Toot! Annie, what'cha gonna do now?
Toot! Toot! Annie, what'cha gonna do?
Toot! Toot! Annie, what'cha gonna do now?
There's a storm there a-brewin'
and you cannot get through!"

Big Annie was not about to give in.
She put her hands on her hips and in her big voice she said,
"I'll tell you what I'm gonna do. I'm gonna pull it myself!"

"Yourself?"

Her friends could not
believe it. "Annie, you can't
go. You'll never be able to
pull that barge
to the children of Natchez in
time for Christmas Day."

"If you help me," Big Annie
said, "I just know I can do it.
When I get tired
all you have to do is
sing me a work song."

The birds said, "We know a great work song, Annie.
We'll sing it for you."

The fish said, "We'll sing it for you, too!"

Then everyone shouted,
"We'll sing it for you, too, Annie!"

Then they all sang:

Heave Ho! Pull the boat, Big Annie

Heave Ho! Pull the boat, Big Annie

Heave Ho! Pull the boat, Big Annie It's

somethin' that you've got to do

"With a work song like that," Annie smiled,
"I know I can do it! Now, don't forget.
Whenever I get tired, you sing me along."

Big Annie waved goodbye to her friends in New Orleans.
She had 150 miles to go.
She picked up her rope and started singing her song.

"In the town of Natchez, all the little children,
Their mommies and their daddies,
they all know I'm pullin'.
Steps are gettin' faster,
remember all the children.
It's somethin' that I've got to do."

Big Annie traveled all morning.
Her friends, the birds and the fish,
traveled along, too.

Big Annie pulled and pulled for 50 miles.
It was time for lunch,
but Annie would not stop.

"The sun smiles down,
tummy is a-grumblin'.
100 more miles, time it is a rumblin'.
Cannot stop, even if I'm hungerin'.
It's somethin' that I've got to do."

Big Annie's arms ached.
"I'm gettin' tired," she said.
"Sing it for me, now."

So all her friends sang.

"Heave Ho! Pull the boat, Big Annie!
Heave Ho! Pull the boat, Big Annie!
Heave Ho! Pull the boat, Big Annie!
It's somethin' that you've got to do."

Soon the storm clouds gathered and the skies grew dark.
The rain began to fall. Big Annie pulled slower and slower.

The fish said, "Don't worry, Annie. We'll help you.
We'll push you along."

The fish pushed with all their might while Big Annie sang.

"The rains come down, splashin' on the water.
3 o'clock, we've gotta make it faster.
80 more miles pullin' up the river,
It's somethin' that we've got to do."

At 6 o'clock, the winds began to blow.
They were so strong that they kept pushing
Big Annie back. She pulled and pulled.
She had 60 more miles to go.

The birds could see that Big Annie was in big trouble.
"Don't give up, Annie," they called as they flew down.
"We'll help you! We'll pull you along."

Lightning and thunder crashed around them.
Big Annie's feet began to drag in the mud.
"I don't think I can make it to the children of Natchez
on time," Big Annie cried.
She pulled her barge slower and slower.
She was so tired.

Then, just as Annie was about to give up, the rains stopped.
The storm was over! It was almost dawn.
She still had 30 more miles to go.

The people along the river's edge called,
"Come on, Big Annie. You can do it!"
The birds and the fish cried out,
"Don't give up, Annie. You can do it!"

Big Annie looked at her friends' worried faces
in the early morning light.
At last she smiled.
"I'll try," she said, "but you all have to help me."

She picked up the rope and they all began to sing.

"Heave Ho! All those little children.
Heave Ho! They all know you're pulling.
Heave Ho! Remember all the children.
It's somethin' that you've got to do."

In the town of Natchez all the children were waiting.
Their mommies and daddies were waiting too.
Everyone was standing on the dock...even the mayor.

As the sun rose, they saw Annie in the distance.
Everyone shouted,
"Come on, Big Annie! You can do it!"

They sang as loud as they could.

"Heave Ho! Pull the boat Big Annie!
Heave Ho! Pull the boat Big Annie!
Heave Ho! Pull the boat Big Annie!
It's something that you've got to do."

Their singing rang in Big Annie's ears.
She pulled faster and faster.
Big Annie would not stop until she pulled her barge
right up to the children of Natchez standing on the dock.
Everyone cheered and shouted, "Hooray!"
Big Annie made it in just in time for Christmas Day.

"Thank you, everyone," Big Annie said in her great big voice.
"I pulled that boat through the wind and the rain,
but I never could have made it
without you all singing me my song."

The mayor of the town stood up tall and said,
"Thank you, Big Annie! We're going to make you famous
all over America. We're going to give you a new name.
We're going to call you ANNIE CHRISTMAS!"

Big Annie laughed and said, "I like that!"

Up and down the river the boats blew their horns!

"Toot! Toot! We're gonna call you Annie Christmas.
Toot! Toot! We're gonna call you somethin' new.
Toot! Toot! We're gonna call you Annie Christmas
'Cause you pulled that barge and you got the toys through!"

"Toot! Toot! We're gonna call you Annie Christmas.
Toot! Toot! Now the children can play.
Toot! Toot! We're gonna call you Annie Christmas
'Cause you got the toys through
in time for Christmas Day!"

Then ANNIE CHRISTMAS gave her great big smile and said, "Yes! With the help of my friends, I got the toys through in time for Christmas Day."